A day in the life of
BARRY BEAN

Graham Aslett

Graham Aslett.

This book belongs to:

_____

It was March 22nd, Barry Bean was very excited to start his new job.

Thanks to those disciplined days working out in the Beanaysium, Barry was the strongest, most confident and fittest bean. That's why Barry was to be the first inside the silver tin.

It was up to Barry to make sure all the beans were poured when the time was right.

No matter when or where it was, not one bean should be left behind.

Graham, the person who lived at number 1 Tidlo Terrace, was hungry. Luckily, he had 6 silver tins of beautiful baked beans in the cupboard.

Barry heard the cupboard door creak open, his heart was racing!

This was going to be Barry's big day...

Or so he thought...

It was a different tins turn.

Barry was disappointed. So close and he knew it. Perhaps tomorrow would be his day.

To Barry's amazement, he heard the cupboard open again. Just 5 hours later, his tin was picked!

All of the beans were asleep but not Barry. He was ready and waiting!

After what felt like a billion baked bean years, Barry heard the tin open.

"STEP BACK FROM THE TOP OF THE TIN" Barry bellowed.

The baked beans were buzzing.

It was time.

As the lid opened a slither of light crept into the tin.

Barry was so happy and all of the beans were bouncing up and down with excitement.

On Barry's count they were to jump head first in to the boiling pan. "3... 2...1... GO!" All of the beans were cheering.

Barry looked down and puffed out his chest, it was his turn.

"3...2..." Just as he was about to jump, he heard a faint voice coming from behind him. "Help me." "Please help me."

Barry looked over his shoulder, to his horror he saw something move.

He ran to where the sound was coming from and there trapped behind a big blob of tomato sauce was a frantic, very scared bean.

Barry looked back at the tin lid, the light getting smaller by the second. This was supposed to be Barry's destiny. It was now or never.

If he tried to get them both out, he wouldn't make it in time.

With all his strength Barry pulled the stuck bean away from the sticky tomato sauce.

He picked the bean up and ran towards the light, he was running out of time.

All of a sudden, they were hurtling through the air in darkness.

Barry held on tight to the rescued bean but the silver tin was already on its way to oblivion.

Graham had thrown the tin into a black plastic bag.

Barry thought he was born for this day but now he didn't know what to expect. He wasn't trained for this. He was - quite rightly - told the silver can should be recycled and not just thrown into a black bin liner.

They had no idea where they were... but they were not alone.

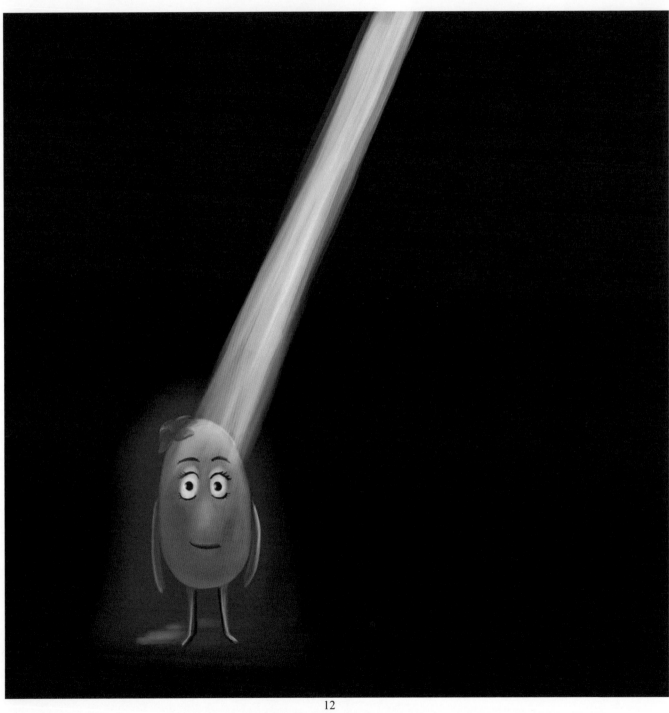

It was then that Barry realised he hadn't even spoken to the rescued bean:

"Hi, I'm Bean. Barry Bean. My mission was to get every bean out of the tin but I failed. I'm sorry".

"You saved my life", the rescued bean replied.

It was at this very moment, Barry noticed that the bean he saved was in fact a lady bean. And not just any lady bean but the *most beautiful* lady bean he had ever seen.

"My name is Betty bean, thank you for saving me."

It was dark and smelly inside the black bag.

As Betty clung onto Barry's little arm, they wondered where they were, how to find the exit and who else was living inside this black prison.

"Why don't we wait until the morning?" Betty whispered.

"The human beings are sure to put something else in the bin and maybe leave some light" Barry agreed.

It was difficult to sleep that night.

They awoke to a noise in the distance. It was Graham, as predicted, sluggishly slurping his breakfast. Suddenly, silence.

The top of the bag opened and in poured Graham's bowl of Bran flakes. Barry and Betty couldn't escape the cold milky gloop raining down on them; they didn't know what it was but Graham certainly didn't seem to like it!

They could now see their surroundings. There was a banana skin to the left and a deep dark cave to the right.

"Can you hear that noise?" Betty asked but Barry was distracted.

"I'm sure I've just seen another bean; I'm worried he is injured" Barry replied.

"Before we look for the bean, we need to find a hiding place, everything we see will be hungry" Betty cried.

Despite Barry going to the beanaysium, he was very little. Bigger than most beans but still very small. Betty held on to Barry's hand tightly; they were too tiny to be seen but if they were spotted, who knows what could happen.

"Who is that hiding behind the banana skin?" shouted a strange voice from the darkness.

The beans froze. Was that question meant for them?

All of a sudden, a wiry little arm reached across Barry's shoulders.

"Hi guys, don't worry. We won't hurt you. My name is Dingo and I'm a soldier beetle. There are 4 of us!" With that, 4 huge figures with mullet-like helmets, full metal jackets and lots of tiny legs appeared.

"Come with us and we'll make sure you are safe" sang Dingo.

"It's a trap!" shouted Betty.

"Oh, come on, we can work it out" the beetles sang in unison.

"Look, try to see it my way. When I was younger, so much younger than today, I never needed anybody's help in any way" they continued.

"So, go on, let us help you," said Dingo.

The beans cautiously followed the beetles in to a cave.

"Like I said I'm Dingo, this is Gorge, this one is Gone and that one is Tall."

"When did you all get here?" asked Barry.

"YESTERDAY!" the beetles tunefully crooned.

"We all like to play music" said Dingo.

Dingo beetle seemed to be the boss as he was the only one who had a seat. A few songs later, Betty and Barry started to relax. The beetles promised to keep the beans fed, watered and safe whilst in the black bag. They all agreed that Barry and Betty should settle down for the night and leave in the morning.

Barry let Betty have the best bed in the bag; a small bottle top with a tiny cover made from a bumble bee's yellow and black fur coat.

As he tucked Betty in for the night, a wave of exhaustion flooded over him. He made his way to a small piece of toast, which the beetles had given him. You see, they knew how much Barry longed to be on the breakfast table. "What a nice gesture" thought Barry.

Within seconds Barry was asleep, happily dreaming of his days when he was just a seed....

He remembered when he was a tiny, tiny seed, leaving the farmer's fingers into the prepared trench where all the young ones started their training. He loved it!

When the ditch was covered, it was lovely and warm. He felt safe in there. It was two weeks before Barry's seed began to develop. Very soon he was big enough to let the bees pollinate his flower. His body grew and after 3 months he was ready.

The lorry took him and his friends to a big factory in the North of England.

When that day came, Barry was bouncing with excitement. He was the very first bean out of over 2 trillion beans to reach the big drum of tomato sauce.

It was finally time to become a baked bean.

As the biggest bean, Barry was perfect for the role of Bean Tin Marshal.

Barry slept like a baby bean. It was as if he was back in his tin snuggled amongst the other beans. He woke up stronger than ever.

Barry was grateful for the fur coat that covered and protected Betty.

That didn't stop him feeling sorry for Bobby bumble bee though; poor Bobby was only looking for a way out of the kitchen.

The beetles said that he was killed after he'd got stuck on the windowsill and Graham had swatted him.

All Graham had to do was open the window and let Bobby bee go, instead he ended up in the black bag as well.

Barry was determined they wouldn't end up like Bobby, he would save Betty and himself.

Barry and Betty's disappearance became front page news.

It was all over the *Baked Bean Times.*

Many knew of Betty's beauty and it was rumoured that Barry was trying to impress her. They said that's the reason he spent time in the beanaysium.

This wasn't true of course; millions knew that Barry was a good bean.

After thanking the beetles for yesterday, Barry and Betty set off on their journey.

They hid behind plastic yogurt pots and old sausages.

Big blue flies flew overhead also on the quest for freedom.

Finding an escape route is all Barry and Betty could think about.

"AAAAAAAAAHHHHHHHHHHHHHHHHH!" screamed Betty.

"WHAT WAS THAT?" shouted Barry.

"Oh, I thought I saw you yesterday" said Barry.

"*Pouvez-vous m'aider?*" the bean replied.

"Pardon me?" said Barry.

"He wants help" said Betty. Barry looked shocked.

"Yes, I can speak French" Betty said, rolling her eyes at Barry.

"*Je me suis perdu*" said the bean. "He has lost his way" translated Betty.

"I'm sorry, I don't speak French" said Barry.

"It's okay, I speak a little human English" the bean continued. "My name is Mr. Hari-Cot, I too am a lost bean. I was pushed off a plate and I landed on a newspaper. I was trapped because the paper was folded. Hours later I was thrown into the black bag."

Suddenly it went dark. Graham had obviously tied the black bag so absolutely nothing could get out.

As Graham walked, the bag started to swing and caught on a rose bush.

The tiny hole was getting larger and larger and when Graham tossed the black bag into the big rubbish bin it tore open. He was too lazy to go back and change the bag, instead he tried to hide it amongst all of the other black bin bags already in the rubbish bin.

The spiders, beetles, woodlice and flies began to make their way to the light. Mr Hari-Cot tried to get the insects to form a queue.

"Children and females first" he shouted, in his French accent.

"Followed by anyone who has been here a long time."

To Barry's surprise, Betty turned to him and said "I'm not going anywhere without you, you saved my life. I will only leave you when we hit the saucepan". Barry was speechless but Mr Hari-Cot shook his head. He wasn't sure about Betty.

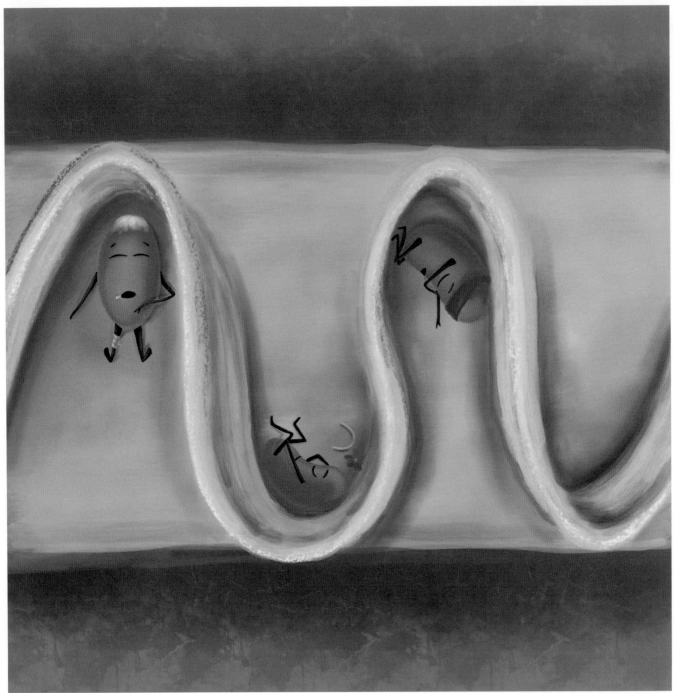

Barry was thrilled to see the beetles making their way through the mess. "Hello, Good Bye, Good Bye, Hello." Their singing was nonstop!

He watched as the queue got longer and longer; they weren't getting out anytime soon. Barry came up with an idea! He went to work making somewhere for them to sleep in a half-eaten banana skin.

None of them slept very well, they didn't want breakfast nor did they want to BE breakfast.

So, they stayed alert and made their way back to the hole that opened yesterday. There was a huge mess and 100s of insects trying to get out.

Barry, Betty and Mr Hari-Cot stuck together and discussed their next move. Barry and Betty were ripe and edible so could still have a chance of completing their mission and fulfilling their dreams.

The plan was to use the worms and old noodles as long fat slimy ropes. They would jump and swing to freedom.

Poor old Mr Hari-Cot wasn't anywhere near fit enough.

The 3 beans returned to their banana-skin base.

Somewhere in Barry's mind he knew he had heard the name Hari-Cot.

It was then Barry realised that he was talking with, perhaps, the most famous bean in the world.

This bean was a legend.

Of course, Hari-Cot! Hari-Cot Beans.

Barry knew he had to save him!

As did Betty who was already forming a plan.

Wasps have never been anyone's favourite. All they seem to do is irritate people, they buzz around the top of your orange juice and then put their head in the hole of the bottle.

If they manage to get out of the bottle, they head for the jam jar and once they're in it, you'll probably never see them again.

If, miraculously, they survive the mighty jam jar, it won't be long until they decide to bang their heads on the window a couple of times, repeating the process again and again before wriggling belly up on the windowsill.

Betty, however, was starting to wonder if these so called *"horrible"* black and yellow stingers could help. The wasps may be irritating but when compared to a bean they are slick and fast with a long body.

Betty was aware of the wasp's reputation but she knew you should never judge a book by its cover. She was determined to befriend these wasps; surely, they are not as nasty as everyone thinks!

Mr. Hari-Cot was not going to be able to walk far.

Barry made him a set of crutches out of a couple of matchsticks.

The 3 of them made their way to the end of the queue hoping to bump in to a wasp or two.

The first wasp they met was called Wally.

Unfortunately, Wally was too busy playing in a cola can, they could only see his head and a tiny bit of his body sticking out of the top, the cola can looked very sharp.

Wally disappeared into the can and Betty assumed he had gone back to bed.

Out of the darkness, a black and yellow flash landed right in front of Betty.

It was the Queen wasp; "who are you and why are YOU walking with match sticks?"

"We've lost our way and Mr Hari-Cot is very frail. I am Barry and this is Betty."

"Yes, I've seen your sort before, Baked Beans, aren't you?" the wasp replied.

"Yes, and we are really glad we met you" said Betty.

"Why? Nobody likes us! We never mean to hurt anyone though" exclaimed the wasp.

"I like you and I trust you; I really wouldn't bother you if we didn't need your help," said Betty.

"We spend our short lives trying to help others but sometimes we get it wrong and like you, not all of us are nice. I'm sure you have bad beans too." "Of course, we do," said Betty. The wasp asked how they could help.

"Well…" Barry explained how they'd been dumped in the dustbin and that he was still holding onto the hope of making their saucepan dream come true. He also mentioned how he rescued Betty. The big wasp listened intently and very soon they hatched a plan to get Barry and Betty back in to the kitchen and rush Mr Hari-Cot to Waspital.

This was a chance to improve their reputation and the big, clever wasp knew it!

Bean BC news was well aware of what was going on. Millions of beans were sat watching the tv, all hoping and praying Barry and Betty managed to make it to the saucepan in time.

Back in the bag, the beans were making progress in the queue.

All of a sudden, 10 wasps came flying in to view in the shape of a triangle. The noise they made was nearly louder than the beetles.

The queue parted just like they had practiced. The wasps kept their wings buzzing, it was *magnificent.*

Queen wasp was leading and very much in charge. This trip demanded that Mr Hari-Cot would travel on the front wasp as he was going to Waspital to get help. Number 2 and 3 were to carry Barry and Betty.

With her wings still fluttering, Queen waspy knelt down as Barry and Betty helped Mr Hari-Cot board the first flight. They used a long staircase which the wasps had made using their own bodies.

It seemed they were experts. Lead by the Queen, they took off one by one.

FREEDOM!

They had made it out of the bag.

The screaming and clapping from the others was so loud.

Barry and Betty waved goodbye.

It was only a short trip but for some reason the wasp force were flying really slowly.

Except for the Queen as she needed to get to Waspital and fast.

Graham had no idea what was to happen that morning.

It was a nice day and he opened his window. A man of habit, he chose beans for breakfast.

There were 7 wasps in a circle on the edge of a large sauce pan.

Graham didn't really like wasps so he started to shoo them away but they just kept coming back.

Barry and Betty were approaching the window along with the two wasps that had carried them there.

Graham opened a silver tin and poured the excited and noisy beans into the sauce pan. The 7 wasps hovering around the hob were distracting Graham so he couldn't turn the heat on until Betty and Barry had made it to the pan.

Barry was dreaming of jumping; he was now the hero of millions of beans. He stood on the edge of the pan with the whole bean world watching and waiting.

They had finally made it.

The wasps flew away and the heat went on.

Everyone cheered as Barry and Betty stepped up to jump.

IT WAS TIME.

Even Mr Hari-Cot had made it back from Waspital and was dancing on one leg and waving.

A huge spoon came in to the pan, all the beans raised their arms begging to be chosen first! "Eat me! Eat me!" they cried with excitement. It wasn't long before Barry was eaten.

Graham didn't eat all of the beans. Some were left in the pan, including the very beautiful Betty. Mr Hari-Cot realised she must have let go of Barry's hand at the last minute and once again hid behind the tomato sauce.

Mr Hari-Cot never found Betty that day but wondered constantly what had happened to her. Bean world adored her, but Mr Hari-Cot wasn't so sure...

Printed in Great Britain
by Amazon

13781536R00029